Moose Tracks

MARY CASANOVA

SCHOLASTIC INC.

New York Toronto London Auckland Sydney
Mexico City New Delhi Hong Kong

ISBN 0-439-16595-4

12 11 10 9 8 7 6 5 4 3 2   0 1 2 3 4 5/0

Printed in the U.S.A.   40

First Scholastic printing, January 2000

To my children, Eric and Katie, and my best
friend and husband, Chas, with love

A special thanks to Avi, Marion Dane Bauer, Lois
Anne Berg, Andrea Cascardi, Pam Conrad, Jean
Craighead George, Dayton O. Hyde, Ted Hall,
and Jane Resh Thomas, who offered insight and
encouragement along the way

A grateful acknowledgement to U.S. Department
of Fish and Wildlife Service specialists Doug
Goseman and Dave Schad and to Department of
Natural Resources game wardens Lloyd Steen
and Dave Rorem

MARY CASANOVA is a recipient of grants from
the Arrowhead Regional Arts Council through
funds provided by the McKnight Foundation, and
from the Minnesota State Arts Board through
funds provided by the Minnesota state legislature.

CHAPTER ONE

Other boys took their shotguns out alone, why couldn't he? Seth stared at the glass doors of the gun case, trying to see beyond his lean straw-haired reflection, which looked back, challenging him, accusing him of being a coward.

"C'mon, open it," Matt said, leaning against the back of the couch in his gray sweats. He passed a football back and forth between his hands, fingernails chewed short. "It's no big deal."

Seth's lungs felt compressed, his hands sweaty. Except for the grandfather clock tick-ticking in the corner, the pine-board living room was quiet, heavy with his father's disapproval. "Easy for you to say," he said, rolling the small brass key between his fingers. "Your dad's not a game warden."

If Seth were like half the other kids in the county, he'd probably take his shotgun into the woods whenever he felt like it. He wouldn't worry about it. Instead, he was expected to obey the law and wait two more long years before he could take his shotgun out alone, without his dad.

It wasn't fair!

It was like setting a big bone between a dog's paws and only letting the dog drool on it. Why did Dad even bother giving him a shotgun last month when he turned twelve if Seth could never use it? Seth had done his part. He'd completed firearm-safety training and was ready to go, but now Dad was always too busy. Did he think Seth could wait forever? Did he even care?

Seth drew in a deep breath.

Slowly, he inserted the key, turned it, and opened the cabinet doors. He pulled out his shotgun and ran his hand along the smooth, polished walnut. It felt good in his grip. Weighty. Solid.

He turned to Matt, who gave the football a spin between his hands and smiled. Without a word, the boys grabbed their jackets and headed out the back door.

In the chill autumn air, Seth and Matt kicked wormy crab apples as they passed the faded red barn, then hiked beyond the pasture into the woods. With his gun carefully angled toward the ground, Seth felt part of something great, like an ancient ritual, a test of his strength and bravery.

Crunching over decaying leaves of aspen, birch, and maple, the boys scanned the moss-covered forest floor as they followed a trail that wound around jagged rock outcroppings, wild-rice lakes, and stands of Norway pine.

A mile from home, Seth spotted huge tracks.

He squatted and touched the deep depressions, long and cleft-shaped. He'd never seen moose tracks so close to home before. A small set criss-crossed the larger set.

Seth looked up to see Matt, in his new green-and-gold jacket, already yards ahead. He'd follow the tracks with his horse tomorrow. Alone.

He hurried to catch up.

They neared the towering white pine, a majestic tree spared from early logging days. Once, after they'd tried to measure the tree's girth and found it wider than two boys could wrap their arms around, they named it after the strongest of Greek heroes, Hercules.

As they walked beneath the tree's massive spreading branches, Seth spotted something moving in the underbrush. It stopped abruptly.

A rabbit.

The boys froze.

Except for white flecks of hair on its face, the rabbit's coat was brown, blending perfectly with the fallen leaves. Only its nose moved, twitching.

Seth pulled off his right glove, slid his finger behind the trigger, and lined up his sight with the rabbit. He eased his shaky finger back on the cool steel.

The rabbit didn't budge.

Seth waited. He wanted to make it fair.

A twig snapped.

The rabbit leaped.

Squeezing the trigger, Seth felt the powerful kick of the shotgun against his shoulder. The rabbit spun in the air and let out a high-pitched scream. A penetrating scream like that of a young child in pain.

Seth stared. His stomach felt knotted, his throat

tight. The rabbit flopped against the ground, its legs moving spastically. This wasn't like the time he'd gone partridge hunting with Dad, where bird shot exploded into a quiet puff of feathers.

In a few seconds, the rabbit lay still.

Seth held the gun toward the ground, but didn't move.

Matt elbowed him in the side. "Hey, you're not done yet."

"I know," Seth said quietly.

From his jacket pocket, Seth pulled out his red Swiss Army knife and flipped open the silver blade. He knelt over the rabbit. Its dark eye stared out into nothing. He grasped one of the rabbit's front paws, still warm, and quickly dropped it.

The woods grew darker.

He picked up the limp rabbit by its foreleg, carried it to a flat rock, and stretched its paw over the stone. As he pushed his knife down into the joint, the bones crunched and separated. The sound made him sick, but he couldn't stop now, not with Matt standing there. Trying to look away, he sawed at the rest of the skin and tendons, and finally, cut the foot off clean.

He'd done it. Glancing up at Hercules, Seth

thought of all the great hunters who had walked these woods before him. At some point, each one had his first hunt, an important hunt that somehow launched him from boyhood into manhood. For Seth, this was his. And it seemed fitting to have got his first rabbit here, beneath this lofty pine. And with only one shot.

He picked up the brown furry trophy in one hand, the gun in the other, and stood. A sense of power filled him.

"All right!" Matt said, slapping him on the back. "You did it!"

"Yeah," Seth said, a little uncertainly.

The boys started down the trail, but Seth turned and walked back to the rabbit. Its eyes were already clouding.

Lifting it by its velvety ears, he tossed it as far as he could from the trail. With the toe of his leather boot, he kicked dried leaves and dirt over the blood-stained rock and then headed home.

He didn't want his dad to find it.

CHAPTER TWO

Seth woke to a high-pitched scream, but it was only the wind. In his fist, he clutched the rabbit's foot. Outside his dark window, the wind threatened to rip the cedar shakes from the farmhouse, howling low and long like wolves before a hunt.

A rustling sound came from the kitchen.

Seth blinked at his clock's glaring red numbers: 4:49. His parents couldn't be up this early.

The paw was dry; he'd baked it in the oven last night while his parents were at their childbirth class. The fur felt silky soft and the green yarn he'd wrapped around the joints had held. Sure, he could have bought a rabbit's foot from the Craytons' drugstore in town, one on a key chain, but it wouldn't have been the same. This one was his. He'd earned it.

Pushing back his flannel sheet, Seth walked down the carpeted hallway. The glow of the kitchen light stopped him short. With the paw cupped in his hand, he peered around the corner, just far enough to see who, or *what*, was in his house.

Seth flinched, nearly dropping the paw. A man with mangy black eyebrows and beard sat at the table pulling leather boots over wool socks. "Mornin'," the man grunted.

It was his father.

"I didn't—I wasn't sure it was you, Dad," Seth said. Undetectable beneath the disguise were his dad's blond hair and clear blue eyes.

Seth slipped into an oak kitchen chair, rested his chin in one hand, and with the other hand eased the rabbit's foot under the table, out of view.

"I try to keep 'em guessing," Dad said, tightening his boot laces. His tone became serious. "Got a call from Ray last night about a couple of poachers."

Ray, the only other game warden in the county,

often joined Seth's family for supper, especially after times when the men worked late together. Those nights, they shoveled in their food like soldiers returned from the battlefield, sharing their stories about searches, ambushes, and arrests—a world Seth longed to be part of. "Don't worry, Seth," Dad would say. "Someday when things slow down, you and I'll go hunting; then you'll have a few stories of your own."

Seth squeezed the rabbit's foot and reminded himself that he'd finally stopped waiting for *someday*.

"We know they've been going after black bear," Dad said, "but we haven't been able to catch them red-handed yet."

"Matt's dad hunts bear," Seth said, remembering the black bear that had dragged their metal garbage can, with the handle in its teeth, all the way across the road into the ditch next to Matt's farm. Seth often wondered if that was the same bear Matt's dad shot this fall.

"With a license, one bear is legal," Dad said, "not dozens. Anyway, Ray got a lead that these poachers are after moose, too. Apparently, some wealthy Texan wants a mounting of a moose cow and calf."

"How'd you find out about that?"

"Through a taxidermist that's been helping us out. It might be just the snare we've been looking for."

Seth wanted to tell his dad about the moose tracks, but if Dad found out about the shotgun, he'd be in trouble. He chewed on his chapped lower lip.

"Disgusting what some people will do for money," Dad continued. "And wouldn't you know it—this year has already been tough on moose."

Seth rested his head on the table, yawned, and rubbed the strands of rabbit hair between his fingers. "How so?"

"Winter ticks—pretty strange," Dad said, reaching for his mug. He sipped his steaming coffee. "The ticks thrived and latched on to the moose. Then, when the moose tried to rub the ticks off, they rubbed off half of their hide as well and couldn't survive the cold." He shrugged his wide shoulders. "Lost half the population in just a year—and not only here in northern Minnesota. Maine had troubles, too."

Strapping a leather holster with a nine-millimeter automatic pistol to his tall frame, Kevin

Jacobson looked like he could handle just about anything. And as a game warden, he did. He arrested people for catching too many fish, for shooting too many deer, and for trapping without a license. It was the game warden's job to confront them with the law, usually alone in the woods, eye to eye, gun to gun. And with his two rules, Keep honest and Never quit, Seth's dad wasn't the kind to ever back down from a job.

What would his dad think about Seth's taking out the gun yesterday? Seth slid deeper in his chair.

His dad took another sip of coffee. "I've been after this feisty old snake Clancy for years. He's living somewhere on state land. Had him cornered a few years back, but then lacked enough solid evidence to nail him. He has a way of disappearing when I get close. He can't go against the law forever, though. Eventually it'll catch up to him."

Seth closed his sweaty palm tighter around the rabbit's foot. If his dad found out about his breaking the law and shooting the rabbit, what would he do? Ground him for a month? Throw him in jail?

Seth stood up in his baggy plaid pajamas, his arms behind his back. Maybe, he thought, he could show his dad just how much he was changing. If his dad would just give him a chance. "Can I go with?" he asked.

"Too dangerous," Dad said with a laugh, then began putting on his bulletproof Point Blank vest.

Seth felt his throat burn. His dad hadn't even given it a second thought! He'd just brushed him away like a fly on his shoulder. Like the stepson he actually was. It had never bothered Seth before, but now with Mom expecting, it felt like everything was changing. This would be "their own" baby.

"Dad," Seth pleaded, hoping that maybe his dad would change his mind, maybe bend the rules, just this once. Why couldn't he understand how important this was? "Please?"

"Hey, Seth. I've gotta hustle before the roads get too icy." He squeezed Seth's shoulder. "Besides, you have schoolwork. Sorry."

"But it's not fair!" Seth said, pulling away. "I'm old enough!"

"That's not the point," Dad said, looking straight at him. Then he spoke more slowly, as though Seth were a child who didn't understand. "This is my work. You know I can't just bring you out there. Besides, you could get hurt." He zipped up his canvas jacket. "Be a help to your mom. I should be back by dark." Then he left.

Seth walked to the living room and sat in the bay window. A clump of bare birch trees shook like skeletons in the wind. As Seth watched his dad leave in his Ford pickup, his stomach felt tight, tight as his clenched fists.

He understood all right. Maybe his dad didn't come right out and say it, but he probably still thought of Seth as just a stepson, just the three-year-old he'd inherited when he married Seth's mom.

He padded back to bed, put the rabbit's foot back under his pillow, and burrowed under his covers. The paw was more than a trophy. It symbolized something important, but what? Strength? Bravery? Certainly, it proved he wasn't just a boy anymore. Seth knew it, and Matt knew it. Still, something about the paw nagged at him.

He knew deep down his dad would never approve, would never understand. But then, why should Seth care? Kevin wasn't his *real* dad anyway.

CHAPTER THREE

As the hallway phone rang, Seth pulled his plaid comforter up over his head, waiting for his mom to answer it. It was always for her on school days.

Two years ago, when his mom suggested his being home schooled, the idea seemed weird. But the fifty-five-minute bus ride to school was slower than a night crawler on pavement. And in winter, when the sun merely peeked over the treetops, going to regular school meant leaving and returning in the dark. At times, he missed his friends, but at least now he could sleep in a little longer.

The ringing stopped and a gentle knock sounded

on his door. Mom peeked in, her wavy brown hair not yet brushed, her denim maternity dress looking tighter than ever across her belly. "Good morning," she mouthed as she handed Seth the portable phone, then stepped out, closing the door behind her.

"How'd your paw turn out?" It was Matt, but his voice sounded lower and scratchier, without its usual high energy.

"Fine," Seth said and reached under his pillow for the paw. He held it up and examined it. "It dried out before my mom got home," he whispered. "She would have hit the ceiling if she'd known it was in the oven, so I made some chocolate chip cookies to disguise the smell. Anyway, all she smelled were the cookies. Especially the burnt ones."

Matt laughed. "Good thinkin'."

"Hey, what are you doing home on Friday?" Seth asked.

"Lousy sore throat. My dad ordered me to rest up. He'll bring me in at lunchtime on his way to the gas station so I won't miss tonight's game."

"Maybe it'll be canceled," Seth said, watching the wind whip snow sideways across the yard, feeling it seep in through the cracks along the old window frame.

"I hope so, because tonight's game is against the Hawks, and they're tough," Matt said. "Sick or not, my dad will make sure I'm there."

"What do you expect? You're his star quarterback," Seth said, picturing Matt's dad standing up in the first bleacher when everyone else was sitting down, cheering full volume for the Cougars. Maybe next year, when Seth was in seventh grade like Matt, he'd go back to regular school and join the team. Maybe then Dad would show some interest.

Matt cleared his throat. "I'm going back to bed."

"Talk to you later," Seth said, and clicked off the receiver.

His mind turned to the moose tracks he'd seen yesterday. Maybe if he could track them, pinpoint their location, then he could prove to his dad he had the skills of a true woodsman. The wind might make tracking difficult, but he hoped it wouldn't be blowing so hard in the woods. Maybe he could gain information about the moose that would help his dad nail the poachers. It was worth a try. He'd make his dad so proud of his tracking skills that he'd have to take notice.

Not many boys would be brave enough to track moose, especially when they were in a rut. During the moose's mating season, a bull moose might charge anything, even a locomotive. He'd have to be careful.

Seth tossed the rabbit's foot in the air toward the ceiling and, feeling a thrill or excitement, caught it in the palm of his hand. He'd show his dad.

He jumped out of bed, turned on the aquarium light, and flicked in a few flakes of food. His two angelfish, Spike and Spinner, glided to the top. When they'd eaten the neon tetras Seth had bought with his own money, Seth had wanted to flush them down the toilet, but he'd got over being mad at them. Sometimes, life wasn't fair.

He threw on a turtleneck, green sweater, and jeans, tossed his comforter up over his pillow, shoved the paw into his pocket, and glanced in the mirror. His hair was sticking straight up in back like turkey feathers. What a dork, he thought.

At the kitchen table, Seth's mother was sitting with a pillow behind her back, her paperwork cluttering the table. Though she only worked ten hours a week doing home visits for Social Services, Seth hoped she wasn't expecting him to be the babysitter when the baby was born. He'd already decided. No way.

Seth eased past her toward the closet. "I'm going to exercise Quest," he said.

"Okay, sweetheart," Mom said. "But when you come in, it'll be time to get to your schoolwork. Today's test day and—"

"I know, I know," he said. Did she have to remind him of everything? "And my name's Seth."

She looked up, her hazel eyes warm and caring, too caring.

Turning away, Seth grabbed his hat and gloves from the closet. He used to be able to talk easily with her. Often, when Dad was away late, Seth would sit on the kitchen counter and talk with Mom nonstop, or together they'd stay up late watching a movie. But not lately. Maybe it came from being together too much, but Seth felt himself pulling away. He needed to stand on his own feet. If he tried to explain to her how he needed to go into the woods today, alone, to track the moose, she wouldn't understand. She'd say it was too dangerous and try to talk him out of it.

"Something else bothering you?" she asked, setting down her pen and resting her hands on her belly.

"Yeah," he said as he zipped up his red down jacket and yanked on his wool hat. "Everybody!"

He closed the door hard behind him. The wind stung his cheeks and ran down his neck like cold skinny fingers. Scrunching his shoulders, he hurried to the old barn.

The pungent smell of hay, oats, and manure met him as he stepped inside. Once used for dairy cows, the barn now housed a tack room, grooming area, and two big box stalls. Quest whinnied. Seth could hear him pawing at the dirt floor.

"Patience, fella," Seth said. "Breakfast is coming."

Grabbing a handful of oats from the bin, Seth went to Quest's box stall, where his four blue ribbons hung, faded like late October asters. The chestnut gelding pressed his muscular chest into the stall boards and buried his warm muzzle into Seth's hand, tickling as he mouthed the grain. When Quest finished, Seth looked at his slobbered hand.

"Hey, thanks," he said with a laugh, and wiped his hand on his jeans. "Friends like you, who needs enemies?"

As Seth curried and brushed down his horse, his cat rubbed her black hair up alongside Seth's leg and purred like a small engine. "Been mousing, Midnight?" Seth asked, as she weaved in and out of Seth's legs. He bent down and scratched her head, then placed her on the stall board. Gracefully, she walked along its edge, jumped down, and disappeared behind bales of straw.

Seth threw a blanket and saddle on Quest's back, straightened the cotton girth, and weaved the leather strap though the girth's silver ring. In his bare hands, he warmed the steel snaffle bit, then gently adjusted the bridle over Quest's ears.

"Come on, boy," he said as he led his horse outside and swung up into the soft leather saddle.

CHAPTER FOUR

As Seth rode out from the barn, wind hit his face with a stinging slap and lifted the long amber hairs of Quest's coat. Sleep and snow filled the air. For a second, Seth almost turned back, but instead he yanked his cap over his ears, huddled into his jacket, and clicked his tongue.

In the woods, the dense pine and balsam slowed the wind to a brisk breeze. Seth inhaled deeply. The earthy smell of autumn was gone and replaced with pure air that tingled his nostrils.

As he passed a moss-covered bank in the woods, he remembered when Max, his old cocker spaniel, had gone nuts barking at this spot. "What's the matter?" Seth had said, walking up behind. Max kept yipping and sniffing up to the edge of the hole until he disappeared, yanked right into the dark hole. Two seconds later he came flying out with a big black head glaring after him. He didn't stop running until he got home. Max must have disturbed the bear's sleep. Probably served him right.

And Seth remembered when dumb old Max had come home with a muzzle of porcupine quills last summer. Dad had pulled most of the barbed needles out of the dog's skin with pliers; the ones he couldn't get out, the vet cut out. And after all that pain, Max was hit by a car a week later. Didn't make any sense.

Keeping his eyes on the snow-dusted trail, Seth rode a mile or so to the west past Hercules, examining prints left mostly by rabbits and deer. Seth stopped for a moment to watch a red fox, its tail an outstretched feather duster, bound across the trail and vanish in the undergrowth. Then he rode on.

No sign of moose tracks anywhere. Perhaps the moose were miles away by now, in search of food. Seth was about to turn back, when the trail curved along the edge of a large peat bog. A stretch of trail too wet to follow in the spring, now it was frozen and carpeted with crunchy pinecones. Brilliant gold tamarack with soft feathery needles surrounded the bog.

Quest stopped abruptly, his ears straight up and his body quivering slightly.

"Hear something, boy?" Seth stroked his horse's neck to calm him. If it was a bull moose, Quest could outrun it; Seth was certain of that. Pretty certain, anyway. After all, Quest was the fastest game horse in the county.

Then Seth spotted the moose cow and its calf. Brown and huge, they grazed in the center of the frozen bog among patches of cattails and long grasses. Uncertain of how the moose cow with her calf might react to him, he backed Quest into the trees, out of view. He let out a silent whistle.

The moose cow was as big as a draft horse, the calf like a yearling. He couldn't wait to tell his dad. For a long moment he watched them, their plodding movements, their knobby silhouettes.

The moose cow's mane bristled up and she lowered one of her ears defensively, as if she sensed something.

The stillness was suddenly shattered by a single gunshot.

Seth jumped in his saddle, and scanned the bog. He couldn't tell where the blast had come from.

Again, one gunshot, then another reverberated around the clearing. Seth's ears rang. His heart began racing. His mouth went dry.

The big cow jumped sideways, then froze, and Seth saw blood on her shoulder. No, he thought, she's been shot! The gangly calf circled around its mother. More blood streamed from the cow's side as she bolted with a wailing bellow, the calf trailing along her flank. Wild-eyed, the cow ran right at Seth.

He couldn't believe it. It was happening so fast, and there was nothing he could do to stop it. He couldn't bear to watch anymore.

Quest danced, but Seth reined him in and backed him farther off the trail, out of the cow's path. Just ten steps away, right in the middle of the trail, the cow's front legs buckled. She went down. The mammoth brown creature moaned, sounding like something from a prehistoric era.

Seth covered his mouth with his glove, his hand trembling. He was going to throw up. His heart pounded wildly, threatening to explode. He was suffocating.

He slid off his saddle and took a step closer to the cow.

Her chest heaved slowly up and down.

"Get up!" Seth wanted to shout. "You can make it!" At least she was still breathing. But there was so much blood. Too much blood.

The calf circled its mother. A small rivulet of red ran down its hindquarter. It nudged its mother's body with its muzzle and made soft bleating sounds.

Quest trembled, anxious to move. A wave of cold panic washed over Seth, telling him to flee, and yet he just stood there.

He heard deep voices.

"I nailed her," said one.

"Yeah, she's not going too far," said the other.

As he stared, blood oozed steaming to the cold ground from the cow's mouth, and she lay still.

Vomit climbed in Seth's throat. His eyes burned. One moment the moose was alive and beautiful, the next it was cut down cold. The rabbit flashed through his mind.

The voices were louder, closer. "She's down all

right. Hit her good—right through the chest."

"Lots of blood, we'll track her . . ."

Seth cautioned himself to flee. Was he crazy? Why wasn't he leaving? Move it! Get out of sight! But the calf, he couldn't let them shoot the calf, too.

Stumbling around the bend, a man appeared, his brown jacket stretched taut over his barrel belly. He smiled at the moose, scrunching his stubble-covered melon face into a grimace of yellowed teeth.

Behind him trotted a well-built younger man, adjusting the flap of his camouflage hunting cap over tufts of black hair. His straight nose jutted out between gray eyes. He lifted his gun at the calf.

Then the men noticed Seth.

"Hey, kid!" the older man shouted. "What the heck are you doin' here?"

"Uh . . . ," Seth said.

The younger man held up his hand. "Hey, sorry, kid. You just startled us, that's all," he said, almost kindly. "I know this must look pretty awful, but we need these animals to feed our families." He lowered his gun. "We didn't mean to upset you. Run along now."

Seth remembered his dad's words. "Only people from Minneapolis or Chicago hunt moose. With licenses costing over a thousand dollars, it's pretty much a rich man's sport." And these guys, with holes in their wool pants, didn't look very rich. But what if they really were poor? What if they needed the meat to survive?

"Didn't you hear?" the old man said in a gravelly voice. He contorted his lips, wadded something up in his mouth, then spit. "We have licenses! Now move it!"

Licenses? But he hadn't said a word about licenses. Suddenly he remembered about the poachers his dad had mentioned. Seth looked at the calf.

"Don't kill the calf, too!" Seth yelled, his voice coming out high and squeaky. He stopped himself, took a deep breath, and tried to lower his voice like his father's, "If I go, you have to promise . . ."

"Promise?" the older man said, eyes narrowing and voice flat. "Sure, we promise." Then he laughed and pointed his gun at Seth.

Seth went numb. He stared at the black hole of a rifle.

"Go easy now . . . ," the younger man said, moving toward the older man.

"Mmm-my d-d-dad's a game warden," Seth

said, the only defense he could think of, the words slipping from his lips before he could take them back. Now he'd given them even more of a reason to shoot.

The man reeled the gun straight up toward the ashen sky and shot into the air.

At the shot, the calf leaped and took off down the trail. Quest reared, but Seth grabbed his reins and jumped into the saddle.

"Hey!" the older man hollered as Seth took off down the trail after the calf. Seth didn't look back.

The calf ran a few feet ahead of Quest, moving fast. It began to limp, leaving light droplets of blood upon the snow. Seth was sure that if he hadn't got between the men and the calf, it would be dead by now. Gradually it slowed down, and finally it stopped running altogether, put its head down, and made a low bleating sound.

"No!" Seth shouted, and nudged Quest into the calf's side to get it moving again.

Halfway home, the calf hobbled off the trail into a marsh of thick cattails. As Seth tried to follow, Quest's legs broke through ice-covered pools. With each step, the horse's muddied legs were released with a sucking sound. Seth didn't want Quest to get stuck if the poachers were following. Besides, he had to get home soon, and he doubted the poachers would follow the calf through the marsh, either. He decided to let the calf go . . . at least for now.

He just hoped it wouldn't return to its mother's body. How long could it last in the woods without its mother to defend it? Would wolves bring it down? Or would the poachers track its blood-stained trail first?

He turned back, and though he wanted to race the rest of the way home, to put as much distance as possible between himself and the poachers, he didn't. Quest's muzzle and chest were already covered with a steamy frost and a lathered sweat.

Seth's chest hurt with a mixture of anger and sorrow. He hated the poachers for what they did, and he felt responsible for the calf. Perhaps, if he could somehow get the calf back to the barn, then the vet could tend to its wound, and he could help nurse it back to health.

As Seth emerged from the woods, he tried to breathe in and out, slow and steady, something that helped calm him before the 4-H horse games at the county fair. Now, he was too keyed up.

He hopped off Quest and led him into the barn. With an old towel, he rubbed the sweat off his horse's back, then he cleaned his hooves, probing around the V-shaped cushion with a hoof pick, searching for small stones. Midnight walked to the edge of the stall boards, purring.

As Seth worked, he heard the bellowing, saw the cow, the faces, the raised gun. He finished Quest's hooves and leaned against the stall boards, grabbing his arms to stop his shaking.

If the hunters were feeding their families, why wouldn't they hunt white-tailed deer, which were far easier to find? Could this guy be Clancy? Quest nudged Seth's leg.

"Okay," he said in an unsteady voice, "I'll feed you." And he tossed a few flakes of hay into Quest's bin, then filled an empty coffee can with oats and poured it into the oat box. He listened to his horse chew, rhythmically, steadily. Somehow the familiar sound helped calm him a little.

CHAPTER FIVE

Walking past the pumpkins and straw-stuffed scarecrow on the back deck, Seth stepped inside.

"Where have you been?" Mom called from the kitchen. The smell of frying bacon filled the air. "You've been gone all morning, and in this weather!"

How could he tell her about the poachers? He sat on the bench and pulled off his boots. His voice came out shaky. "I just took Quest for a ride down the trail."

"If you'd let me know, Seth, then I wouldn't have to worry." She cracked three eggs into a skillet.

"You always worry," Seth said, stepping into the kitchen. He silently toasted slices of raisin bread, smothered them in butter, and poured himself a glass of milk. He didn't feel like talking and carried his plate of bacon and eggs to the study. Where was the calf now?

When he finished eating, he stroked the wood desk and stared absently around the room, at the computer, his two-foot stack of *National Geographic*s, and his collection of old bottles: blue, green, amber, red, short ones and tall.

Mom stepped in. She walked up to Seth and put her hands gently on his shoulders. "Earth to Seth, Earth to Seth. Come in, please. Do you read me?"

Seth sighed. "Roger, I read you."

"All you have are your tests, Seth. Just start."

He sighed. "I know, Mom."

"When you've finished, I'd like some help moving baby furniture from the garage attic into the nursery. The baby isn't due for another month, but I want to be ready, just in case."

"Sure," he answered.

As Mom walked out, Seth twirled his pencil between his fingers, his thoughts returning to the moose calf. If he could somehow lure the calf to the barn, then he could care for it. With the gunshot wound in its hindquarter, and with the sudden cold, it probably wouldn't survive without Seth's help. Somehow, he had to find a way to get it into the extra stall for shelter until it fully recovered.

His eyes wandered to the painting of a deer asleep against a tree, oblivious to the prize-winning buck trotting past. Seth remembered hearing that sometimes hunters clanked old deer antlers together to trick nearby bucks into thinking there's a fight. When a buck came to investigate, either because it wanted to fight or because it thought a doe might be nearby, the hunter would shoot. If it worked for luring deer, maybe it could work for moose, or a moose calf. It was at least worth a try.

He set his correspondence-test sheets on his desk and told himself to get to work. If he worked fast, he could finish his schoolwork early and get back out to the woods to help the calf. He didn't have to wait inside all day for a bell to ring.

Finishing his math and geography sections quickly, Seth plowed through the fill-in-the-blank science questions. When he finished the last question, he set down his pencil, put the test into a white envelope preaddressed to Calvert School, Baltimore, Maryland, and stretched back in his chair.

He looked at the clock. 12:38. Record-breaking time. He was done for the day.

Before going back outside, Seth made himself a peanut-butter-and-banana sandwich and took a big bite. The peanut butter globbed to the roof of his mouth.

"I've never seen Kevin so excited," Mom said on the phone, sitting on the couch in the living room. Birch logs crackled in the fireplace. "Last night at childbirth class he was asking more questions than anyone and taking the coaching part so seriously that I kept laughing when I was supposed to be deep breathing. . . . Rachel, it's just so different. I mean, I would have loved that kind of support the first time around."

Seth gulped down his glass of milk. *First time around.* He tried to picture his mom having a baby all alone at a hospital near the university, without a father nearby who cared. She probably wasn't too happy about it, about having a baby all alone back then. Now it was different. When Dad was home, he spent all his time giving her back rubs with a tennis ball and talking to her belly.

Seth clenched his jaw. He had to get back to the woods. He glanced in the living room at his mom, who was still talking on the phone, then turned toward the back door. Reaching in his pocket, he touched the soft fur of the rabbit's paw to remind himself of his bravery. But was it really bravery to shoot the rabbit? He couldn't think about that now. Quietly, he slipped outside.

Snow swirled around the yard. He wondered where the poachers were now. Most likely, they'd taken some time to drag away the moose cow. But were they out there now, hunting the calf? Seth felt hot with anger. He had to hurry. He had to get to the calf before they did.

In the barn, Seth reached into a barrel and pulled out an apple. He held it in the flat of his hand for Quest, who bit it in half with a chomp, then grabbed the other half with his teeth.

Seth didn't want to wait to warm the bit, so he used the hackamore bridle, the one without a bit, that puts pressure on a horse's head. For extra warmth, he'd skip the saddle and ride bareback.

He grabbed his leather waist pack hanging from

a nail and scooped in a dozen cups of shiny golden oats—the perfect bait for a moose calf.

"Sorry, boy," Seth said to Quest as he opened the barn door, a blast of wind hitting him full in the face. "I hate to make you leave your cozy stall so soon."

Icy branches creaked as Seth rode back into the woods. It felt as if there were fish flopping around in his stomach. He hoped his plan would work.

Circling to the south side of the marsh, where the calf had crossed, Seth found fresh moose tracks that led down a well-traveled deer path into the woods.

Seth hopped off his horse and led him by the reins, following the teardrop tracks down a rocky slope. He slipped over knotted tree roots and fresh snow and found himself in a lowland of cedar.

Stepping over downed trees, Seth stopped next to a large pawed-out mud hole about five feet in diameter. Though he'd read of these mud holes, he'd never run across one. Even half-frozen, it had a strong, pungent smell, like horse urine. It was a wallow, a meeting place for moose during their mating season.

Seth smiled and gave himself a thumbs-up. This

was better than he hoped for. The calf probably had been here before with its mother. Maybe it would return. All his senses were on full alert. He heard the creaking trees, the rustle of a mouse beneath the ice-covered ground, the breathing of his horse. He looked around. A chickadee flitted past.

He was sure the calf was near.

And Dad would be amazed when Seth led him into the barn, with the moose calf in the stall, its wound bandaged. "Saved him from the poachers," Seth would say. Dad would pat him on the back and say, "Best son I could ever hope for," or something like that.

He dropped Quest's reins to the ground.

As Quest searched for blades of grass beneath the snow, his muzzle frosty with cold, Seth found two heavy sticks.

He searched for the right tree and found it just a few yards up the slope overlooking the lowland clearing. The perfect climbing tree, a forked white pine. Using the tree's branches for his ladder, he climbed up and balanced himself on a branch about nine feet above the ground.

Sitting on the branch, his shoulder against the

tree's trunk, Seth started whacking the sticks together, hoping to attract the calf.

Clack. Clack. Nothing.

Clack, clack, clack.

No sound of approaching moose. No deer coming to investigate, either. Seth hit the sticks together repeatedly, trying different rhythms, hitting soft and then loud, fast and then slow, until he was just about ready to give up on the whole dumb idea. Besides, his toes felt numb.

He started knocking his boots together to warm himself.

The likelihood that he'd attract the calf was about one in ten thousand. Maybe he *was* little more than a kid with no brains after all. Why else would someone sit in a tree pounding sticks together?

He gave it one more try—just in case the calf had heard the sound from far off and was traveling closer to investigate, perhaps wanting to be near another moose.

Clack. Clack. Clack.

No movement at all, except Quest chewing on a few weeds.

Suddenly Quest's head shot up. The whites of

his eyes showed. A crashing sound came toward them, the sound of branches breaking under the great weight of something huge.

Something powerful.

CHAPTER SIX

The massive body and rack of the bull moose filled the small clearing. He snorted and blew out short angry blasts of air.

Seth held his breath.

Quest reared and pivoted, then bolted through the woods up the bank toward the trail.

"Quest! Come back!" Seth yelled. He put two fingers to his mouth, ready to whistle for Quest. Then he looked at the moose and hesitated.

The bull moose lowered its rack and pawed at the ground, stirring up a shower of leaves, dirt, and snow. Then it charged after Quest a few feet and stopped.

Walking back toward the clearing, the moose moved nimbly with its huge rack between cedar branches. No animal, not even a wolf, was a match for a healthy bull moose.

As Seth clutched the branch more tightly, his sticks dropped through the tree's lower branches to the ground.

At the sound, the moose turned its head toward the tree, its eyes dark glass marbles. Seth had heard that moose had poor eyesight; he wondered if it could see him now.

The bull lowered its head, its giant rack glistening with snowflakes, and made a low, throaty bellow that reverberated through the trees.

Seth tried to swallow, but his throat was tight and dry. He pressed up closer to the tree trunk and tightened his grip on the limb. The branch creaked.

Seth froze.

The bull snorted and pawed again at the wallow. He walked in a wide circle, head down. Nostrils flaring, the bull pointed his muzzle into the air. He walked over to the tree and scraped his antlers back and forth along the trunk, as if sharpening his equipment for battle.

Seth's heart pounded so hard that he thought it might explode.

For a few moments, the bull stood still, ruler of the forest, then lumbered to the wallow, pawed around the edges, straddled it, and peed.

It seemed unaware of Seth.

The moose backed up a few feet and waited, its shoulders and haunches broad and muscular, beautiful and frightening.

Time stopped.

Neither moose nor boy moved.

Seth's sweaty hands turned icy inside his gloves. His toes felt like rubber. How long would this moose keep him there? How long would it take to freeze to death? Would he just turn solid in the tree, or would he gradually lose his strength and fall from the tree and then get trampled by the moose? This far from the trail, nobody would find him. His body would simply rot into the forest floor.

Snow fell in heavy flakes and melted on Seth's nose and cheeks. Gradually, the moose's back grew a layer of white snow.

Five minutes. Twenty. Maybe an hour.

Seth's face felt tight, as though it could crack like hard taffy.

All he could hear was the bull's steady breathing. He watched it paw at the wallow, circle, then come back to the tree, raking its antlers against the bark.

A twig snapped.

Into the small clearing walked the moose calf, gangly, long-eared, with small dark eyes and a pelt as brown as chocolate. Though it looked too big to have still been nursing, it limped over to the bull and poked its muzzle toward the bull's belly. The bull feigned a charge at the calf but didn't touch it, merely scared it.

The calf jumped back a few feet, its legs so long that it seemed it could get tangled in them, then it walked again toward the bull. This time, the bull lowered its head and rammed the calf, pushing it away from the wallow.

The calf bellowed.

Determined, it walked toward the bull again and nudged its muzzle against the bull's nose. The bull butted it hard in the side with a thud.

Just as Seth was going to yell at the bull, it lumbered off into the woods, as though it didn't have time for such games. Its handsome rack blended in with the branches, and then it disappeared.

Seth let out a breath he seemed to have held for hours.

The calf started off after the bull, then turned back and stood by the wallow, circled once, twice, then lay down. On its haunch was a black splotch of dried blood with a few droplets of red.

Seth winced. He wondered if the bullet was lodged in the calf's leg; if so, it would have to come out. He hoped his plan of getting the calf back to the barn would work. He couldn't just "let nature take its course." Not this time.

After waiting a few minutes longer, he relaxed his grip on the tree, his muscles twitching from having been still so long. Despite the icy, penetrating stiffness in his legs, he inched down until his boots touched the ground. He kept his eyes on the calf, unzipped his waist pouch, and grabbed a handful of oats. Then he crept silently toward the calf. Step by slow step. Perhaps he was crazy, but . . .

All at once the calf gathered its legs and stood up. It was much taller than it had looked from the saddle or the tree. Seth found himself within arm's reach. The calf stared at him.

Seth didn't move, waiting to see what the calf would do.

Then, trembling, he slowly held out the oats toward the calf.

Bringing its muzzle to Seth's hand, the calf sniffed, then blew out a blast that sent the oats flying. It backed away into the trees and stopped, its large ears flicking gently back and forth.

Seth started up the slope, letting the oats drop from his hand.He kept all his movements slow. He didn't want to scare the calf away. Not now. If he couldn't help it soon, it would probably die.

Reaching the top of the slope, Seth tossed another handful of oats in the calf's direction. The calf threw its head back.

Seth worried that he'd scared it. Maybe he was hoping for too much. He couldn't wait much longer; it was getting late.

But then the calf took one step toward the grain, and then another, until it finally dropped its head to the ground and began to follow Seth up the slope toward the trail, limping one step at a time, a safe distance behind.

CHAPTER SEVEN

Seth shook the last oats from his glove onto the snow-carpeted trail. He looked over his shoulder at the calf. With its muzzle down, it pawed at the ground, searched to the left and right, and then lifted its head. Wind blew violently across the top of the pines, but only whispered in hushed tones across the earth's floor.

If only he had more oats, he could lead the calf straight home. For now, there was nothing more he could do. Seth stared at the lanky creature as it stared back at him, reminding him of cows along the roadside. Dumb, innocent eyes.

"About the killing," Seth said aloud. "I promise, I'll get even for you."

Seth's throat tightened, and when the calf flicked its ears and turned away into the woods, he wiped his eyes with the sleeve of his jacket, glad that Matt wasn't around to see him.

Seth swung his arms in wide circles and clapped his gloves together to keep his blood circulating. The chill was in his bones. He couldn't wait to get into a hot bath and warm up. And after a steamy bath, he'd flop down on his soft bed. He quickened his step.

Seth hoped Quest had headed for the barn. A herd animal by instinct, it would be in the horse to run from danger, to fight only if cornered. That bull moose sure scared the wits out of Quest, Seth thought.

A large log jutted from the trail. Once moss-covered, it now had a six-inch mound of snow across its length. Seth realized that he was near Hercules and looked up at the limbs of the stately pine. It seemed alive, as though it held accumulated wisdom from years of being still and watching. Just beyond the tree, somewhere under the snow, lay the rabbit carcass with one missing paw.

Seth felt suddenly confused. The brave feelings he'd had about the paw were slipping away. It didn't make sense. Matt had been impressed with him. And since getting it, he'd stood up to the poachers, faced the bull moose, found the calf. Then why the hollow feeling? And why did it continue to haunt him?

Two black scraggly ravens, perched high in the branches of a decaying birch, cawed back and forth to one another as Seth walked by. He sensed their bullet eyes watching. Ravens, some people believed, were a sign that bad things were going to happen. Scavengers, ravens often fed on the remains of dead animals. But Seth didn't believe the superstitious stuff. Were they there to feed on the rabbit? Were they watching him? Their presence made him feel jumpy. If he let himself, his imagination could easily run wild, but he wouldn't let it. He was too old to get scared by walking in the woods.

With each second, the woods grew darker, a gray curtain pulled down farther and farther. He should have told his mom where he was going.

Seth broke into a run, not stopping until he came out of the woods.

Snow blew across his face and swirled around his boots. The sky was darkening, and Seth figured it must be around five o'clock.

Quest stood beside the barn, tail into the wind.

"So you made it back without me," Seth said. He grabbed his horse's reins, lifted the ice-glazed latch, and stepped into the near darkness of the barn. He reached for the hanging light string. "Did that big moose give you a scare?" he said to Quest.

A voice, menacingly familiar, answered back. "No lights! Over here, kid, before I slit your throat like a strung-up pig!" It was the gravelly voice of the older man of that morning.

Seth's legs turned to putty. He looked into the darkness of the barn. Two shadowy figures stepped toward him from behind the bales. They were the two men he'd met in the woods.

"Be quick," said the younger man. "We don't have all day."

A flashlight clicked on in Seth's face. He couldn't see.

Seth dropped Quest's reins and lunged for the door, but a heavy hand grabbed his shoulder and threw him back against the bales of hay.

"Now listen!" The older man stood over Seth,

holding a glowing red cigarette. Before he could continue, he began coughing, a dry guttural hacking. Cigarette ashes landed in the straw near Seth's feet. "We don't . . . want trouble," he said.

The younger man came up alongside the older man and stared down at Seth.

"We just stopped by to make a few things clear," he said in a voice as smooth as Seth's dentist's. "We're concerned that you might go blabbing about something that isn't your business. You know what I'm talking about?"

The reek of alcohol and smoke pinched Seth's nostrils.

Seth nodded. Quest clopped to his stall, more interested in hay, apparently, than in what happened to Seth.

"You guys gonna kill me?" Seth squeaked.

The younger man raised his eyebrows, and drilled Seth with his eyes.

"I haven't said anything," Seth said. "Not a word."

"That's very good," the man said slowly. He smiled. "Just what we wanted to hear."

"But . . . how did you know where to find me?" Seth asked.

"There ain't too many game wardens to choose from," said the old man. "Besides, seems you were trying to steer the little calf in this direction. So where is it now?"

"I don't know. It ran off," Seth said. He wanted to scream. What were these men going to do with him? "Uh, would you like supper or something?" Seth blurted out, hoping to soften them up.

"I like this kid, Clancy," the younger man said. "Would we like supper? He's real thoughtful. . . ."

Clancy. So these men *were* the poachers Dad was after! A chill swept over Seth. He had to think fast.

"I, uh, could bring out some food," Seth said, hoping they'd let him go inside and that his dad would be home already. Then he'd show these guys.

The old man spoke, his voice a growl. "No, kid. We didn't come for supper."

Seth stared down at the yellow circle of light on the dirt floor.

"We're here," he continued, "to make sure you don't crawl like a cockroach into the light. You know what a cockroach does? Look at me."

Seth forced himself to look at the man's face.

When he did, Clancy turned the flashlight up

under his whiskered chin, creating shadowy streaks across his greasy face. The man smiled, revealing black holes between his teeth. Seth shuddered.

"A cockroach stays where it's dark—like under the stove—so nobody will come along and squish him with their shoe." Clancy coughed, then dropped his cigarette butt onto the dirt floor and ground his heel into it. "Now, you don't want to get in our way, do you?"

"No." Seth shook his head.

The younger man reached down and picked Seth up by his jacket shoulders. He held him for a long second, just staring at him with eyes dark as ice-fishing holes. Then he whispered, "Do you like your family?"

"Yes," Seth croaked.

"Then keep this to yourself, or somebody might get hurt."

The poacher dropped him. As Seth landed on his feet, the man punched him across the side of the face. Seth crashed into the bales of straw.

Everything went black. He couldn't move. His body seemed disconnected from his brain, as it felt in nightmares when he'd try to move but couldn't. Yet he could hear.

"Why'd you hit him that hard, Robert?" Clancy said.

"To scare him good. I don't want to have to come back a second time . . . ," Robert said, "to finish the job."

Clancy lowered his voice. "You mean you'd—"

"Don't give me any grief. I warned you, this operation isn't small potatoes. You're in deep now, whether you like it or not. Let's get out of here."

Their words faded away.

Seth dropped deeper into blackness, free-falling down an endless chasm.

CHAPTER EIGHT

"Seth?" Mom called. "Seth?"

"Mhmmm." Seth tried to reply, but his mouth felt as if it were full of cattail fluff.

The light clicked on.

"Oh, dear Lord . . . Seth!"

Seth forced himself slowly up on his elbows. He looked around the barn. It was no dream.

"What happened?" Mom asked. "Did Quest kick you?"

For a few seconds he couldn't remember where he was. Then it all came back. The poachers. How could he tell her about them? If the poachers found out, they'd come back and finish him off for sure. He didn't want to lie, but he didn't have a choice.

"You're bleeding!" she said, kneeling by his side. "Oh, Seth . . ."

"I'm okay, Mom," he said, pushing the words from his lips. "Really. I just, uh, was out riding and I fell off Quest—right onto my face. Stupid, huh?" His head throbbed. "I came back, put Quest into his stall, and then, um . . ." He sat up, turning his head slowly. Midnight walked over his out-stretched legs. Seth's neck felt stiff as a two-by-four. "Guess I just fell asleep."

"Pretty bad fall," she said.

Seth wished she'd just keep asking questions until she pried the truth out of him. But how could he tell her now?

"Something sharp tore your cheek," she said quietly, stroking his head.

Seth brushed away her hand, slowly stood up and wiped his hand across the dry blood on his cheek. He knew the poachers' faces. He could iden-tify them, but what if he did? Would they really come after his family? "I must have hit a rock. I'm all right, really. It's no big deal," he said, beginning to feel dizzy.

Seth's mother pulled Seth under the light and looked at his cheek, her eyebrows bunched together. "You need ice, and possibly stitches, too."

She held the barn door open. "Let's get in the car and head to the hospital," she said, and sighed. "I wish your father was home."

After his mom applied some ice and a large bandage to Seth's cheek, they drove to the hospital. All during the half-hour trip, Seth felt awful. He thought he could stand up to the poachers, but look what had happened instead. They'd knocked him out cold, could have killed him. And if he talked, they'd come back. How could he have thought early this morning—it seemed like years ago—that he was ready to team up with Dad? The words, "You might get hurt," pounded in Seth's head. Dad knew Seth was no more than a wimpy, snivelly nosed kid.

Walking down the long gray corridor of the Great Falls Hospital, Seth hoped he wouldn't need stitches. He turned a corner with Mom and passed the admitting office and gift shop. Both were closed. As they passed patients' rooms, his mom raised her forefinger over her lips.

Moaning came from one room, and in another Seth saw a patient walking around—the back strings of the man's gown barely holding it closed.

Three nurses chatted at the desk.

"Hello." The blond nurse smiled, revealing two deep dimples. "What can we do for you?" She looked at Seth's mother first, her eyes resting on her bulging belly. "Is it time?"

"No, I certainly hope not," she laughed. "I'll be ready in a month—not a day sooner."

"Ah, under those bandages, I bet," the nurse said, pointing to the large flesh-colored bandage on Seth's cheek.

"He has a nasty gash on his face," Mom said.

Seth looked down. He knew what the next question was, and he knew he was going to have to lie again.

"What happened?" the nurse asked.

"Uh, I fell off my horse."

"You were riding on a day like this?" she asked with a laugh.

"Yeah." Seth suddenly felt exhausted. He went back to studying the square floor tiles.

"Doesn't make sense to me, either," Mom said. "It's hard to figure boys out sometimes."

Seth looked up quickly at his mom. She was smiling. If only she knew the truth of what had happened. She wouldn't be smiling then. He looked back down at the ground again. feeling completely alone.

The nurse held out a clipboard for Seth's mother to sign. She asked a hundred questions about insurance, allergies, and family medical history. What did family medical history have to do with a cut on his face anyway?

"And the father's medical background?" the nurse asked.

"Biological father's background unknown," Mom said quietly.

Father's background unknown. Seth's face went hot. It made him feel like a nonperson.

He glanced at his mom, her belly protruding beneath her cape. At least the baby would have a real dad. But suddenly Seth felt angry with himself. Maybe he was only a stepson, but by trying to prove himself to Dad, he'd put his family in danger, real danger.

He put his hands in his pockets. He felt the fur of the rabbit's foot. His mind raced. He pictured the poachers breaking into his house . . . moving in the darkness . . . heard his mother scream . . . What would he do then?

He shuddered.

"This way," the nurse said, interrupting his thoughts.

Seth and Mom followed her to a small white room.

"The doctor will be right with you," the nurse said.

Mom sat in a chair, a magazine in her hands.

Seth hopped up on the examining table and brushed his fingers across his bandaged cheek. Even a light touch sent streaks of pain to his jaw. His cheek burned. He looked around the room.

Seth focused on a poster. At first it seemed just a haze of boxes, but as he looked more closely, he realized he was looking at hands—six hands in six large squares. Seth read the information at the top of the poster. "When a body appendage is lost," the poster said, "the following precautions must be taken."

The poster showed a hand that had been cut off in a farming accident. It explained, step-by-step, what to do with a hand or arm so that it could later be surgically put back on the person. "Wrap it in paper towel wet with saline solution," Seth read. He pictured adding salt from the shaker to water.

"Place in a sealed plastic bag." He pictured putting it in a Ziploc bag. Plunk.

The doctor walked in, a man looking more like a clown than a doctor. His shoes were at least a size thirteen, and he wore a Hawaiian-print tie under his white doctor's coat.

"Dr. Gekko—Friday night—usually a busy night," the doctor said in a rush, scratching his thin gray hair. "So, let's check you out." He walked to Seth and whisked off the bandage. "A slight laceration, bruised, but it won't take much to make sure it heals properly." He poked around. "Mmm . . . five or six stitches should do it."

Seth forced himself to sit up straight.

As the doctor gathered his equipment, Seth kept his eyes on the wall in front of him.

"Lie back," the doctor said. "First I'll give you a shot . . . numb you up."

He tensed up as the doctor pulled on surgical gloves. From the corner of his eye, Seth saw the needle.

He felt a pain in his cheek. The shot was over.

Next, Dr. Gekko held up a white cloth with a three-inch hole in the middle. "Just relax," he said, and placed it over Seth's wound. "Try and think of something else. Warm ocean breezes, music, Jamaica, or maybe the Bahamas . . ."

Seth thought of the poster. "Keep it cold," he'd read. "Refrigerate if necessary." Seth pictured putting the hand into his refrigerator. Disgusting. His head began to spin. In his mind, the hand turned into a paw—a rabbit's paw. Weird.

Before Seth knew what was happening, the doctor's voice drifted farther and farther away, and he felt himself go limp.

He fainted.

CHAPTER NINE

"Fifteen miles per hour!" Mom said, gripping the steering wheel. "At this rate, it's going to take us all night to get home."

Seth thought about the wounded moose calf. Was it smart enough to find shelter? Could it survive in weather like this? Was Dad still out trying to find the poachers?

"That happened to me once, Seth," Mom said.

"What?"

"Fainted."

"Oh, that," Seth said, feeling pretty stupid.

"I was watching my little brother, your uncle

Peter, have an IV needle put in his arm. He had pneumonia, and they couldn't find his vein. They kept poking around for it, and I kept watching. Next thing I knew, I was on the floor in a heap," she said. "It happens to lots of people."

"Yeah," he answered. He knew she was trying to make him feel better. But drawing attention to it didn't help. The fact was, he'd fainted over nothing.

It seemed he'd been more scared in this one day than he'd been in a lifetime. More than the time he'd run into a bear and her cub in the apple orchard. More than before any horse show. More than when he took out the shotgun with Matt. But guys shouldn't faint when they get a few stitches or when they look at a medical poster.

Snow blew hard across the road, hiding the dividing line and pelting the windshield. The wipers pulsed back and forth, unable to keep up with this snow. A gust of wind sideswiped the car.

"This is terrible," Mom said, and hunched toward the windshield. "What a night. . . ."

The wipers ticked back and forth.

When they hit a patch of ice, the car fishtailed sharply back and forth. Seth felt his stomach rise to his throat. He grabbed the armrest.

"Oh, Lord," Mom cried out. "Hang on. . . ."

The car jolted off the smooth pavement toward the ditch. His mom swerved the car back on the road again, but this time too far to the other side. They were in the opposite traffic lane.

Car lights loomed toward them through the white-speckled blackness.

"Hit the brakes!" Seth yelled. He closed his eyes and grabbed the armrest more tightly.

Just as the oncoming car came closer, his mom regained control of the station wagon and eased back into the right lane, slowing the car to a crawl.

"Thank God we didn't get hurt," Mom said. "That was too close." She let out a long breath.

"Why didn't you hit the brakes?"

"If I'd slammed on the brakes," she said, "it would have put the car into a spin. I'll feel better when we get home and stay there. No more hospital visits tonight, okay?"

"Promise," Seth said, scratching lightly at the tape around his bandage.

For a while, they didn't speak.

Seth thought of what his mom had said: *biological father's background unknown*. It sounded so cold. Incomplete. Seth reached in his pocket. He turned the paw around and pressed the sharp toenails of the rabbit's foot into his palm until it hurt.

"My real dad," he blurted out. "I want to know about my real dad." There. He had the courage to say it.

Mom kept her eyes on the road. She began tapping her fingers on the rim of the steering wheel, but said nothing.

"Mom?"

She cleared her throat and let out a sigh. "I've always wanted to tell you," she said. "I just didn't know when you'd be ready, when you'd want to know. . . ."

Seth waited.

"First," she glanced quickly at Seth, her eyes pained, then back to the road. "You have to know I've never for one moment regretted having you, Seth. Never." She paused. "My only regret was, well, the way you were conceived, that you didn't start out with a father to help raise you those first few years. I wish now that I had *waited* until I met and married Kevin. I can never change that, can I?"

"No," Seth said, waiting.

"But when I held you for the first time, all red

and wrinkled and beautiful, I suddenly realized that life is a miracle, a gift."

Seth swallowed hard. "But my real father," Seth asked, trying to sound casual, as though it all didn't really matter. "What's his name?" His heart pounded.

"He said his name was Michael O'Henry."

Michael O'Henry. The name sounded friendly, almost hopeful.

"I met him when I went on a college ski trip in Steamboat Springs," Mom said. "He said he played hockey for the Minnesota North Stars, and maybe that impressed me then."

The North Stars! His biological father was a professional hockey player? Incredible. Was he still playing? Could Seth go to one of his games sometime, maybe meet him afterward?

"I was foolish," Mom continued. "I let myself get swept away by him, not thinking about the future, not even thinking about protection at the moment. I wasn't thinking at all. And later . . . ," she paused, rubbed the back of her neck.

Seth waited for her to continue, clutching the paw even tighter in his pocket.

". . . when I found out I was pregnant, I tried to

contact him, to tell him he was the father. I thought he should know. But the North Stars' coach told me they'd never had a player by that name. Never heard of him."

"You mean . . . he lied to you?" Seth couldn't imagine that someone would lie about their name. After all, if a person couldn't be honest about their name, then they probably couldn't be trusted with anything. He turned his face slightly toward Mom. "So then what happened? You were just on your own?"

She nodded. "I'm sorry, Seth. I wish I could tell you he was a man you could look up to."

Seth felt numb.

The wipers ticked steadily back and forth.

Maybe he'd never fully admitted it to himself, but he must have hoped that someday he'd meet his real dad. Now, it was as if a door had slammed in his face. Yet, if his real dad wasn't someone Seth could respect—someone like Kevin Jacobson— then maybe it was best the door had closed.

"Mom," he said. "It doesn't really matter."

"But of course it matters," she said, "otherwise you wouldn't have asked. If it makes you feel better, you inherited his good looks."

"I was hoping it was my slam shot on the ice."

They both laughed.

"Any more questions?" Mom asked.

"Not right now," Seth said, reaching across the seat and placing his hand on her shoulder.

As the station wagon pulled into the driveway, Seth looked for Dad's truck. It wasn't the first time Dad was gone late, but this night, more than ever, Seth wished he were home.

He wanted to tell Mom about the poachers, but they had him in their grip.

CHAPTER TEN

Water steamed in the claw-foot bathtub, rust-stained from minerals that continually leached from the earth into the well water. Seth soaked his body, absorbing heat like a lizard on a sun-drenched rock.

It was 10 P.M., and Seth wondered if his day would ever end. He tried to forget everything, but the poachers' faces loomed before him. One with a face like a cabbage head, round and colorless. The other, long-nosed like a wolf, with steely eyes. A shiver zigzagged through Seth's body despite the hot water, which had turned his legs beet red.

What made him madder than anything was that he didn't have any evidence against them. Nothing. Who would believe a twelve-year-old kid?

He avoided getting the stitches on his cheek wet as he put his head back and washed his hair. Then he stepped out, grabbed a towel, and looked at himself in the cabinet mirror. What a mess! One eye was puffy and half-closed, just a small slit to see through. His cheek was bluish gray with a touch of green and swollen with five small stitches across his cheekbone. The face in the mirror didn't even look like his. And it was older, he thought, more serious.

He moved closer to the mirror. His expression reminded him of Dad's, the angry look that crossed his face when he talked about deer shiners, poachers who use a bright spotlight in the middle of the night to hunt. Blinded by the brightness, the deer freeze and then the shiners shoot. Maybe some poachers are trying to put food on their table, Seth thought. That might be forgivable. But for others, poaching must be a sort of game, like shooting ducks at a carnival booth and taking home cash.

The more he thought about the poachers, the madder he felt. Beyond being a threat to Seth, there was a rottenness about them that posed a threat to the woods and everything in it.

He pounded his fist on the sink. They can't just come in here—on our property—and threaten me! Rough me up! He couldn't let them get away with it. It was wrong, and they deserved to be arrested. He couldn't let them scare him into silence. He owed it to the moose calf, he owed it to himself. As soon as his dad got back . . . if Seth could just hold it together until his dad returned, then maybe . . . Maybe what? Tell Dad what happened, only to have him go out and get himself shot?

Seth dressed and joined his mom in the kitchen. He plugged in the popcorn popper. Over the whir of the popper, he heard the phone ring.

Mom answered it, stepping into the living room.

Seth finished popping a bowl of fluffy white kernels and unplugged the popper.

"Dad called," Mom said, putting the phone back down. She picked up a blue-striped dish towel and began drying a pot. "He won't be back tonight."

Seth felt himself sag inside. "What?"

"He said he's working with Ray and moving in

on a big arrest of bear poachers. I'm just relieved to know he's not in a ditch somewhere."

"Bear?" Seth couldn't believe it. Dad was completely off the poachers' trail. "But he said he was going after moose poachers!"

Seth's mother leaned her back against the sink and lightly massaged the top of her round belly. "I don't know what he's doing exactly, Seth. He didn't say very much. . . ."

"He'll never catch them now," Seth muttered.

"C'mon Seth, you know he doesn't make an arrest every time. If you're implying that he's not doing a good job, if that's what your tone means . . ." She stared at Seth and adjusted her hairclip. "Seth, you've been acting strange all day. I know you wanted to talk about your real dad, maybe that's it. But is there more that I should know about?"

He wanted to tell her, but his throbbing cheek reminded him of the trap that held him. "I was hoping Dad would get home," he said.

"I know," she said. "Me too."

Grabbing the ceramic bowl of popcorn, he double-checked the lock on the back door, then headed downstairs to the basement, where he watched TV and slept most Friday nights. Only this night hadn't been his usual night of late movies and popcorn. Hardly. Cross-legged on the old plaid couch, he mechanically ate his popcorn, one kernel at a time. When he finished the bowl, he rolled out a sleeping bag and climbed in. Pulling the pillow over his head, he fell into an exhausted sleep.

He dreamed that he was riding in the woods, without a shirt, and snow was swirling around him, blinding him with its brightness.

Suddenly Quest broke into a gallop, and Seth fell off the saddle, his leg getting caught in the stirrup. Quest dragged him endlessly over logs and streams, scraping him up and down rocky ridges until Seth's back was bloody. Time and again, Seth tried to reach up and cut the stirrup loose with his knife, but no matter how hard he tried, he couldn't reach it. Finally, Quest stopped short.

Seth yanked his foot free and tumbled to the ground.

He looked up. The bull moose was there, its rack higher than the trees, standing above him, piercing him with eyes dark as a starless night. Seth tried to scream. The bull thrashed its hooves in the air. Seth had to be quick. With an instant jerk of action, he rolled clear of the sharp hooves pummeling down at him.

Seth woke when he hit the basement floor, tangled in his sleeping bag, clammy with sweat.

CHAPTER ELEVEN

The basement floor felt as unforgiving as an ice rink. As Seth clambered back onto the couch, yesterday flooded across his mind, fully waking him with a chill.

He dressed fast and climbed the stairs. Maybe the poachers had him scared into not talking, but that didn't mean Seth would let them get the moose calf without a fight. He had had good luck getting the calf to follow him before. This time would be even easier. He had to hurry, before the poachers found the calf first.

He looked at the clock above the fireplace. 7:07. The house was still quiet.

Crumpling newspaper under dry birch logs in the fireplace, Seth struck a match and watched an amber flame lick at the wood. He blew at the base of the pile, sending the flame into an explosion of heat, then closed the glass door. Now Mom wouldn't have to get up so early to start the fire. And if he was lucky, this time he might get back before she'd even miss him.

Saturday. He wished he could call Matt and tell him everything, then ask him to come along. But if he called Matt, maybe he'd be putting his friend at risk, too. He'd have to go alone.

Seth went to the kitchen, made himself a double portion of instant strawberry oatmeal, and shoveled it into his mouth. Dad's boots and jacket were nowhere to be seen. He still wasn't home. Seth topped off breakfast with a Snickers bar from the cupboard and put on his jacket.

He checked his jeans pocket. The rabbit's foot was still there, silky soft. What did the paw really prove? Did it prove anything at all? It did nothing to help loosen the knot he now felt in his stomach. Filling his lungs with a deep breath, he told himself that he had enough courage to return to the woods; then he pulled on his cap and headed out the door.

In the middle of the backyard, tree swallows fluttered around the birdhouse, trying to get out of the wind. But bird feathers stuck out of the two round openings. The birdhouse was crammed full.

"Better head south soon," Seth said.

He shoveled snow away from the barn door, then kicked a chunk of ice to hold it open so that the swallows could find shelter.

"Anybody in here?" he shouted, working up the courage to enter the barn.

Quest rose to his legs, stretched his neck over the stall rail, and blinked.

"Good morning, old pal," Seth said, relieved to be alone this time.

Midnight walked toward him, then stopped and stretched in a low bow. She purred and wrapped herself through Seth's legs. First, Seth filled the cat's food dish, then he removed the insulating box from the barn's water spigot, filled her water dish, and brought Quest a bucket of fresh water. Quest slurped noisily.

"That's very rude," Seth said in his mother-knows-best voice.

When he went to the bales, something caught his eye. Sticking out between pieces of golden straw was an unfamiliar watch. Seth picked it up and studied it, running his fingers over it as though it were a rare archaeological treasure. It was a Timex with a hairline crack running across its face from the two to the seven. The weathered leather band had apparently come loose with the blow.

Seth lightly brushed his hand over his stitches. No wonder he had been cut. But now he had evidence. With this, his dad might be able to pinpoint the owner and make an arrest. He turned it over in his hands, hoping to find an inscription on the shiny back side. A name. There was nothing except a few numbers around its rim.

He set the watch on the stall boards and entered Quest's stall, tossing him hay. "So you ran home without me," Seth said, "left me out there alone with that bull. Wasn't very brave of you."

The barn door creaked and Seth jumped. A rush of cold wind blew into the barn. He wondered what he could use to defend himself.

Grabbing the pitchfork, he hid in a corner of the stall and peeked through a crack in the boards. His body tensed like a twisted rope.

"Seth?" Matt called. "You here?"

Seth stepped out cautiously, pitchfork raised.

Matt stood in the doorway in his green-and-gold jacket, his sweatshirt hood over his head. Under his arm he hugged his football.

"Am I ever glad to see you!" Seth said as Matt closed the door behind him and walked to Quest's stall. Seth leaned the pitchfork in the corner, then sat down across from Matt on a bale of hay. He drew an X in the dirt with his boot heel.

"Our game was canceled last night," Matt said, pacing back and forth. "We would have played, but the other coach didn't want to take his team on the road. And I'm feeling better."

Seth didn't answer. The last thing he had on his mind was football. He had to get going.

"Game's postponed till next week," Matt continued, stopping momentarily to lean over the stall and stroke Quest's side. "I went to bed early, then woke up at five this morning, couldn't sleep. I saw footprints to the barn, so I thought . . ." Matt faced Seth. He wrinkled up his face into a confused smile. "Hey, what the heck happened to you? Did you go out for football and not tell me about it?"

"You wouldn't believe me if I told you," Seth said, his cheek and jaw feeling sore when he talked.

"Well?" Matt asked impatiently.

"Poachers," Seth blurted.

"What?" Matt said. "C'mon. Did I hear you right?"

"I probably shouldn't even tell you, Matt. I mean, just by opening my mouth, I might be putting your life in danger."

Matt was still for a moment, then he began nervously thumping his football.

Seth didn't smile.

"Poachers?" Matt repeated. "You're serious, right?"

Then Seth told Matt everything, from when he'd first spotted the moose tracks to when the poachers had waited for him in the darkness. As he talked, the wind rattled the old barn, trying to shake it apart. "And this," Seth said, holding out the watch, "is the only evidence I have."

Matt studied the watch. "Geez. Think they'd really come back?"

Seth pointed to his cheek and raised his eyebrows.

"Yup, I think they probably would," Matt said, nodding. "I think you better tell your dad right away even if they threatened you. He'll find a way to arrest those guys."

"I don't know what to do," Seth said. "My dad's not home yet anyway." He kicked at the dirt. "I can't wait around for him to get back. Matt, I don't expect you to understand, but I have to get back to the woods."

The wind howled outside the barn. Seth looked up. Two swallows, white breasted with long dark coattails, flew in through the crack in the door and perched on the overhead rafter, as though to eavesdrop on the conversation below. At least he'd helped a few swallows.

Grinding his heel into the dirt, Seth said, "That moose calf might still be alive, and if it is, I'm not going to let those guys blast it."

Matt tossed the football to Seth. "I don't think you should go out there alone."

"Well," Seth said, throwing the ball back to Matt. "Want to join me?"

Matt looked up at the birds, then at Seth. "As my dad would say, 'It goes against my better judgment, but okay.'"

Seth tried to smile, but smiling tugged at his stitches. "Mind riding double?"

CHAPTER TWELVE

Under a blanket of gray clouds, the boys rode into the woods, Matt's hands clamped on the edges of the saddle seat behind Seth. Except for the creaking of ice-glazed branches and snow falling in clumps from pine boughs, the woods were still. They rode quietly for a long time.

"I wish you'd taken my advice a long time ago and gotten a four-wheeler," Matt said behind Seth. "This isn't exactly comfortable, but at least Quest is warm.

"What are we going to do if we run into those poachers?" Matt asked.

"They'll be gone," Seth said, trying to sound sure of himself. "They wouldn't have left the moose cow out here where wolves could get it. I'm sure they're long gone."

As they neared the bog, Seth stopped Quest and listened. Sparrows fluttered overhead. He nudged Quest forward.

"The spot's right up here. I'm hoping the calf will be hanging around the bog up ahead. Maybe the cow's scent will keep it near."

The moose cow's body was gone and yesterday's bloodstains were now buried under snow. The air smelled wet and bitter.

"So this is where you ran into the poachers, huh?" Matt said.

Seth nodded. He looked around the bog. It was as though it had never happened, and Seth almost felt as if he'd imagined the whole thing. Then he noticed that fresh moose-calf tracks crisscrossed the area ahead. The calf had returned to the site.

"See those tracks, Matt?" Seth said. "See? The calf headed that way." He lifted Quest's reins and headed southwest, following the tracks and clusters of brown droppings. The tracks led them along the edge of a stream that trickled in hushed tones beneath a layer of ice, and followed the base of a high ridge trimmed with bare rock, juniper bushes, and Norway pine.

The fresh wet snow made the tracks easy to follow.

"We're getting closer," Seth said quietly as Quest skidded down a small ravine.

A half-hour later, the tracks led them to a clearing on top of a rounded rock ridge. In the middle of the hill sat a strangely shaped mound of snow, almost like a snow-covered beaver dam or giant anthill.

As Seth nudged Quest closer to the mound something clicked against Quest's horseshoes. Seth lifted his leg over the saddle horn, then jumped off the saddle and kicked around in the snow with the toe of his boot. He discovered old bottles and scraps of rusted metal, including a wire hoop that had once been a barrel stave for a wooden keg. He picked up a small bottle, crusted black inside.

"An antique whiskey bottle," he said, brushing off the snow and dirt and reading the glass lettering. "I'll add this one to my collection. Neat, huh?"

"Maybe you think so," said Matt, sitting awkwardly on Quest's rump and trying to hang on to the reins.

"Bet this one is fifty years old—at least," Seth said. He put the empty bottle into his jacket pocket and stepped toward the mound.

Just as he stepped forward, his foot broke through the outer edge of the mound. Seth flung his arms backward toward solid ground, propelling himself away from the shaft.

"Hey, are you okay?" Matt asked, sliding off Quest. He gave Seth a hand up.

When Seth regained his footing, he knelt near the mound and looked at the small dark hole that had opened where his foot had gone through. His heart was beating fast.

"Yeah, I'm okay," Seth said. He listened to the clink of debris as it fell into the pit below. "That was close."

"This mound must cover an old mine shaft. My dad said there were lots of hematite mine shafts around here from the early iron ore days, but he never told me about this one. He said miners used to cover these with timbers and then pile garbage on them—to keep hikers away. Guess the timbers are rotting through." He took a deep breath, stood up, and brushed the snow off his jeans.

He grabbed Quest's reins and walked to the edge

of the ridge. Below, a trail curved past the ridge, running west and north; a trail large enough for snowmobiles or four-wheelers.

"I didn't know about this trail," Seth said.

"Me, neither," Matt said.

Prickles ran down Seth's back. If the poachers used these trails, he hoped they weren't around now. Maybe he should turn back. But then he spotted the calf's tracks.

"Matt, look," Seth said. "It's headed that way, down the hill."

"We'll find it," Matt said, then added cautiously, "unless . . ."

"Unless what?" Seth didn't like Matt's tone; it made him nervous. He glanced around.

"Over there," Matt said, pointing to a half dozen large black birds circling above the aspen trees beyond the ridge. "Ravens. Something must have died."

Seth swung up into the saddle, then gave Matt a hand up to Quest's rump.

The calf's tracks appeared to be heading toward the aspen grove. Had the poor calf made it this far, only to become food for ravens?

"I hope it's not what I think."

As Quest traversed slowly down the rocky ridge, Seth leaned back slightly in his saddle. He felt the warmth of Matt's chest against his back. He was glad for his company.

They followed the calf's tracks, which cut over the trail and into the aspens. When the woods became more dense with undergrowth, the boys slipped off Quest and walked.

The ravens' squawking grew louder.

Seth felt uneasy. He had wanted so badly for the calf to make it. He had wanted to see it survive. The tracks led right toward the ravens. Maybe he didn't need to go farther. Wasn't it enough just to know that the poachers hadn't got it? No, he needed to know for sure. He'd follow the tracks until he found the calf.

Yards ahead, in a small clearing beneath leafless trees, at least a dozen ravens were on the ground, squawking as they tore at dark mounds with their beaks.

One raven cawed from a treetop as Seth and Matt approached. The other birds flapped up into the trees, perching above their snow-speckled piles of black, like sentries standing guard.

Seth shivered. What were these dark boulder

shapes on the ground? The whole thing gave him the creeps.

As Seth walked closer, Quest followed behind, prancing and snorting nervously.

Suddenly Seth understood.

It made him sick.

Whoever had killed them, Seth thought, didn't kill them for their meat—they weren't gutted clean. They certainly didn't kill them for their fur.

Matt stepped up behind him. "Ohhh . . . ," he groaned.

Seth stood still, unable to take his eyes off the scene. From what he could make of it, all the bears' paws had been hacked off. The animals were slaughtered for their paws and perhaps a part of their innards.

Seth wrapped his arms tight around his waist. He couldn't believe someone would . . .

He turned to Matt. "Bear poachers," Seth said. "This is their work."

"What an incredible waste," Matt said. "At least when my dad gets a bear, we eat the meat. But this . . ."

"Jerks!" Seth said, angry that anyone could kill bears like that, just slaughter them. And then a thought jabbed him. *He had killed the rabbit and cut off its paw—for no good reason*. He reached into his pocket and clasped the soft fur and bones of his rabbit's paw.

Now it repulsed him. How was it that he could so clearly see the harm the poachers were doing without seeing the wrong of his own actions? He thought about how he'd struggled to protect the moose calf. If the moose calf's life was worth saving, then why not the life of a wild rabbit? Seth felt heavy with shame. The rabbit's foot didn't prove his strength; it only proved his stupidity.

Seth heard something and lifted his head.

A soft bellowing, barely loud enough to hear, came from deeper into the thicket.

"Hear that, Matt?"

CHAPTER THIRTEEN

The bellowing grew fainter, then it stopped.

As the land sloped downward, aspens gave way to lowland brush. When the brush became too tangled, the boys turned from following the calf's tracks to following its sound instead.

Seth held up his hand to Matt.

He heard splashing.

Following the noise, Seth parted the thick weave of branches as he walked and came upon an eight-foot-wide ice-covered stream. In its center, stuck shoulder-deep, was the moose calf, its back covered with snow. Ice chunks and clumps of mud floated in the muddy brown water around the calf's head.

It was clearly in trouble.

The boys stood on the edge of the bank, not saying a word.

For a moment, the calf stared at the boys with its close-set, shiny black eyes, then it thrashed its front legs at the surrounding shelf of ice. Over and over again, it tried to lunge upward, but each time, it merely broke off a chunk of ice and fell back into the water, apparently digging itself deeper and deeper into the muddy bottom of the stream. After several attempts, the calf stopped and drooped its head in exhaustion on the edge of the ice.

How long had it been stuck in the stream? Minutes? Hours?

"C'mon!" Seth cried. "You can't give up!"

The calf bellowed a mournful cry, then started thrashing again.

Seth felt as if he'd cheered it into trying.

He looked around and noticed a large birch branch sticking out from the snow. Grabbing it, he pushed the branch across the ice, hoping to make a bridge or something on which the calf could get a foothold. The calf threw its head away from the

branch. Seth broke more branches from the surrounding bushes and frantically piled them on the
edge of the ice, in front of the calf. The calf shied
back from the branches.

"Come on, fella!" he shouted. "Try harder! You
can make it!" If he only had some rope, he could
hitch up Quest to pull the calf out. And a board,
too. The calf needed something sturdy to climb
onto.

"We need rope and a board!" Seth said.

"Yeah, but from where?"

"From home."

"You're going all the way back?" Matt asked in
disbelief. "It's too far."

"I don't know what else to do," Seth answered,
his voice breaking. Matt was right; it would be at
least an hour, maybe two, before they returned.
"Got any other ideas?"

Matt shook his head, "Nope."

"We've gotta hurry. Wounded like it is, it won't
last long."

Just then, the calf plunged forward. Its hooves
landed on the mound of branches Seth had laid in
front of it. It began to lift itself forward slightly, as
if it might actually get out this time.

Seth backed out of the way, expecting the calf to pull itself up and come barreling out of the water at them.

Instead, the ice cracked away from beneath the calf, and it fell down again into muddy water, its head inches above the waterline.

The calf bellowed once more, a cry that penetrated the marrow in Seth's bones. Seth clenched his fists. Only yesterday he believed he could conquer anything. Now he wasn't so sure.

Seth turned from the calf and walked back through the tangle of brush to Quest, who had his head down, grazing.

"We have to try," Seth said to Matt.

With the two boys riding, Quest danced skittishly past the bear carcasses and bolted out of the aspen trees onto the trail.

"Whoa," Seth said. Against the base of the ridge, he noticed a large piece of plywood, poorly camouflaged with fresh pine boughs. "Hey, maybe we won't have to go all the way back home. See that?"

"What?"

"The board. We could try sliding it under the calf's front legs. It's worth a try."

He knew he had to move fast. If the calf didn't

get out soon, it might get so weak and cold that it would drown before it froze. Matt slid off the horse's back, and Seth swung out of the saddle.

Quest put his head to the ground and pushed away snow with his muzzle, searching for grass.

Seth walked away from Quest, pulled away the branches, then yanked at the sheet of plywood. Behind it he found a three-foot-by-five-foot cavity.

He put his head inside the dark, dank entry.

"Don't, Seth," Matt cautioned. "It was blocked off for a reason."

"I'll be quick," Seth said. "I just have to see if there's any rope." Along the inside rock wall, Seth felt something hard and cylinder-shaped. He tugged at it and it came free. It was a large battery-operated lantern. He pushed the button on. Light filled the rust-colored mine shaft. He stepped back out into the light.

"It doesn't go in very far," Seth said, stepping into the horizontal shaft. About twenty feet ahead, the shaft appeared to dead-end. The lantern revealed little—just a rock-walled passageway with rubble on the floor. "The miners must not have found enough in this shaft to bother going deeper," Seth said. He took a few more steps in and shone the light toward the end of the shaft. "Wait. I take that back."

Seth breathed in the musty air. It wasn't a dead end. Seth craned his neck cautiously around the corner. Instead of being a narrow shaft, the passageway opened to a room. On the far wall were two bunk beds with sleeping bags stretched open on ragged gray mattresses. Boxes, nets, and snares littered the rest of the room.

Seth held his breath for a second, then let it out slowly. "This must be a hideout." He felt as though he were looking the poachers in the face.

"See any rope?" Matt asked.

"Not yet."

"Well, come on. Let me see . . . ," Matt said as he edged around Seth and stopped. Let's look for rope, then get out of here. Fast."

"Gross!" Seth said. Like ingredients for a warlock's brew, dozens of black gourd-shaped things dangled from a wire stretched across the ceiling. "What are those?"

Matt wrinkled up his nose at the bulbous shapes. "Probably from those bears. Gives me the creeps." He started searching around the bunks.

"Look at all this evidence, Matt," Seth said. He

quickly walked around the room. He lifted a wire loop next to a pile of snares. "They trap . . . boy, do they trap." A wolf hide lay on top of a large pile of pelts. Seth quickly thumbed through them—lynx, beaver, otter, mink, marten, fox . . .

He picked up a white plastic bottle and held it under the light. "Look at this! 'Poisonous.' Bet this is how they get their hides." Then he squatted next to another set of boxes and held up a stick of dynamite.

"What would they want with dynamite?" Matt asked.

"Bet this is how they fish, by blowing the fish to the top of the water."

Behind the box of explosives, Seth pulled out a coil of white rope. "All right! Let's help the calf, then we better find my dad—"

He stopped.

The sound of a motor filtered into the interior of the mine shaft. The rumble grew quickly louder, as though it were going to come right in after them. Then the motor stopped abruptly.

"Oh no," Seth said.

Matt's eyes grew wide.

CHAPTER FOURTEEN

A voice echoed off the dank shaft walls, filtering into where boys stood motionless. "Looks like we've got company," Robert said.

"Seems we've been seeing this horse way too much lately." It was Clancy. "Wonder if someone was planning to ride it home?" A laugh. A slap. "Get going!"

Then a gunshot rang out.

Seth shuddered and his eyes filled with tears. Had they really shot his horse? He wanted to run out of the shaft and pound them with his fists. But what good would that do? He had to think of a way to escape.

"Tracks lead right in, Robert. Two sets. I'll bet it's that kid and one of his buddies. Look over here. Hey! They took my lantern, those little—"

"Hey!" Robert yelled from the shaft's entrance. "Bring me the lantern and we won't . . ." His voice changed. "Don't you know," he said more calmly, "that you're trespassing on private property? If you'll just step outside without any trouble, we won't have to press charges."

Private property? Seth doubted that. The county map at home showed that nearly all of the land beyond his house belonged to the state.

"Come on now," Robert said.

Seth was unable to think or move until Matt pointed to the pile of rubble. Between the pile and the ceiling was a small dark hole. Quickly, they climbed up over the rocks. Seth squeezed in first through the opening at the top. "Come on!" he whispered. "They're coming!"

Matt crawled up after him, but stopped halfway.

"My sleeve's caught!" he said.

Seth aimed the light on Matt's jacket sleeve, which was caught on a wood beam jutting out from the pile.

"Slide out of it," Seth whispered. "Quick!"

Matt slipped out of his jacket and yanked it free, then squeezed through the opening toward Seth on the other side of the pile and lay down.

"Shoot, I ripped it! My mom will kill me."

Seth snapped off the light. "Be quiet!" he whispered.

Darkness surrounded them, darkness so black it seemed to press down upon them. Now they were trapped, and the calf wouldn't survive. Seth's own breathing seemed too loud. The rocks felt cold and damp. Footsteps shuffled down the passageway.

"If I had the stupid light . . . ," Clancy complained.

"There's a flashlight in one of the boxes," Robert said, then lowered his voice. "You block the passageway so they don't sneak past us."

Seth could hear Clancy's rattled breathing, footsteps, boxes moving.

Light spilled over the top of the rock pile.

"Where are those little twerps?" said Clancy.

"Scoot back," Seth whispered, fearing that the men might be able to spot the tops of their heads. As they slowly edged down the dark side of the pile, a rock tumbled onto the shaft floor.

"Well, well, well," Robert said. "Only a couple of kids could fit back there."

"Yeah, two kids that'll be the end of *us*," Clancy said, "if we don't do something about *them*. They'll blow us right outta the water!"

"Hey, now, there's an idea," said Robert. "Just like in the war, going after an enemy you can't see."

Seth heard them rustling through boxes. Then the men chuckled in a way that made his blood stop cold. He held his breath.

"I'll grab the pelts," Robert said. "You grab the gallbladders. They're dry enough to ship by now."

Gallbladders, Seth thought. Is that what those funny looking things were? He remembered reading something in *National Geographic* about bear poaching—something about people using bear gallbladders for an aphrodisiac, a kind of love potion. The demand for the stuff in Asia was great, commanding huge sums of money. He'd never dreamed the bear population would be threatened here.

"Got everything to do the job?" Clancy asked in his raspy voice.

"You doubt me?" Robert replied.

The boys found themselves in darkness again. Were they going to use the dynamite? Seth waited. Slowly, he let out his breath.

"Think they'll really leave?" Matt whispered. "Or just wait outside to trick us?"

Then they heard Robert's voice.

"Move the four-wheeler! I'll get them fixed up here."

After a few moments of silence, Robert began counting. "Ten . . . nine . . . eight . . . seven . . ." The counting faded away.

Seth squeezed his eyes shut as he realized what was about to happen. "Matt! Get down and cover your head. They're gonna blow the entrance!"

They waited one more second in darkness.

Kaa-booooommmmmmmm!!!

The explosion shattered the silence and rang through the mine shaft. All around them, rocks fell like a shower of meteorites.

CHAPTER FIFTEEN

Seth's ears ached. Dust filled his mouth and nostrils as he choked and coughed. He touched a throbbing knob on the top of his head. With outstretched hands, he groped in the blackness, uncertain of floor or ceiling. He touched only cold rock.

"Matt?" he said. When he didn't respond, Seth panicked. *What if he's dead?* "Matt!"

"Uhmm . . . ," his voice came as if from far away.

"Where are you?" Seth cried. "I can't find the lantern. Are you all right?"

"Uhmm . . . yes . . . no. My head hurts," he said, catching his breath, ". . . my leg . . ."

Seth crawled toward Matt's voice. He felt the smooth plastic of the lantern, found the button, and turned it on. The rock pile they'd hidden behind had spilled across the floor of the poachers' room.

Matt lay on his back with one leg under rocks. His face was covered with reddish gray dust; a small gash on his forehead dripped blood over his left eyebrow.

"You look pretty rough," Matt said, his voice strained.

"You've looked better yourself," Seth tried to joke back, but he knew deep inside that they were in real trouble—trouble from which they might not escape.

Seth pulled the smaller rocks away from Matt's leg first, then pushed with all his might on the biggest rock.

"Ouuuuch," Matt moaned.

"This one's too heavy," Seth said. "I need to pry it with something." He needed leverage.

Against a wall, he found a two-by-four beam and angled it under the rock's edge, then went to the other end of the beam.

"When I say 'now,' you roll out of the way," he

said as he pushed down with all his weight on the beam.

"Now!" he groaned.

"I'm trying—," Matt said.

"Hurry, or the rock's going to fall back down!"

Matt pulled his leg free, and Seth let go of the timber. The large rock thudded back down where Matt's leg had been.

"Is it broken?" Seth asked.

"I don't think so," he said, exploring his leg, "but it hurts bad."

The tunnel entrance had collapsed with no sign of daylight from the other side.

"They have us in here pretty tight," Seth said. "I wonder how long until we run out of oxygen." What had he got them into? "Wait," he said. "If they can dynamite us in here, why can't we blow our way out again?" He shone the lantern toward the boxes. The explosives were gone. So much for that idea.

"There's gotta be a way out of here!" Seth shouted. "There's gotta be!" He felt panic rise within himself. "Lord," he prayed, a simple prayer coming from deep in his being, "help us."

Seth remembered his mom's words that life is "a

gift." No matter what he faced, even if it was the worst, his life, from start to finish, was in the hands of the Creator. And with that thought, he somehow found a quiet place within himself.

A hiding place.

That was it! Seth scrambled over the leveled rubble. He lifted the lantern. The light illuminated a new shaft directly behind the pile of rock rubble. The explosion had blown the entrance to this once-blocked shaft wide open.

"Matt!" he said, looking into the four-foot-high tunnel. "Take a look!"

Matt stood with all his weight on his right leg. He shrugged his shoulders and hung his head. "It just goes deeper into this hill."

"Well, I'm going to find out," Seth said as he crouched low, picked up the coil of rope, and entered the reopened shaft. Maybe it wasn't the best hope of escape, but at least he'd find out where it led to.

Ten feet in, a rock boulder blocked the shaft, but Seth squeezed by it and kept going.

"Wait up," Matt said coming from behind. "I'm not staying in the dark."

Loose rock fell from the low ceiling. Seth raised a

gloved hand to protect his head. What if the shaft were to collapse and they got buried beneath loose rock? He wanted to turn back, but to what? A blockaded prison? Again, he crawled ahead, feeling the dampness around him.

Plunk. Plunk. He heard the slow drip of water. Plunk. Plunk. Plunk.

Ahead, he saw a rust-encrusted pickax leaning against one wall, as though someone had come down this shaft to work but never finished the job, never came out.

Something feathery brushed across Seth's face. Seth felt crawly. He tried to bat at it, whatever it was, and dropped the lantern. But it was still on his face.

"Hey!" Matt called. "I can't see!"

Picturing a wolf spider the size of a half-dollar, Seth swiped his hand across his cheek. He let out his breath. It was only a cobweb.

"Sorry."

He picked up the lantern and held it next to the low ceiling. He looked back. Matt limped up slowly, his face crumpled in pain.

"You're hurting?" Seth asked.

Matt nodded, biting his lower lip.

Then Seth started off again, moving slower. They rounded a bend in the tunnel.

Ahead, threads of light broke the darkness.

"We did it, Matt!" Seth said.

Through holes as big as nickels, light pierced a wall of boulders. Working together, Matt and Seth tossed and heaved and pushed earth until they had a hole large enough to squeeze through.

Rope in hand, Seth dropped down to the snowy ground next to Matt. Daylight never looked better. Cedar trees concealed their exit on the southern slope of the hill. Beyond them was the stand of birch trees—beyond the birch trees was the calf. Seth listened for its bellow. All he heard were ravens cawing.

There was no sign of the poachers or of Quest.

"Come on," Seth said, and began climbing up the slippery hill. They had to make sure the poachers were gone before they could get the plywood.

As they came over the crest of the slope, they spotted two men below on the west side. Clancy and Robert were strapping a blue tarp over the trailer behind a four-wheeler.

Seth motioned to Matt to crouch low. If they moved quickly and quietly, they could slip away with the poachers still thinking they were in the mine. As they slunk across the top of the hill, Seth saw Clancy turn. Seth and Matt dropped on their bellies.

"Those kids!" hollered Clancy.

"What?" Robert said. "Impossible!"

Seth's heart raced. They'd have to disappear in the woods before the men followed them to the top of the hill. They might have their guns. "Run!" he called to Matt. He felt his fear turn into a power that propelled his legs forward, almost as if they weren't his own.

"We can't let them get away this time!" Robert yelled.

Seth raced past the edge of the old debris pile. He looked back. Matt was limping behind.

He ran back to Matt.

"Put your arm around my shoulder!" Seth said. Matt leaned some of his weight against Seth, and they hurried toward the woods.

"Stop!" Robert hollered, his voice close behind. "That's an order!"

Hobbled together, the boys ran through scraggly sumac toward the woods, until Matt stumbled, falling to the ground.

In that moment, from the corner of his eye, Seth could see the camouflage cap. Robert grabbed Matt by the jacket collar.

"Run!" Matt said. "Get help!"

CHAPTER SIXTEEN

Seth ran through the trees, oblivious to pain as branches scraped his face. He slid down a small hill, scrambled up the next ridge, and tucked himself behind the trunk of a Norway pine. He had to get help, but what if it wasn't soon enough? Shaking, he looked across to the top of the other ridge.

Through the trees, he could see that Matt was on the ground in a heap, looking up at Robert.

"If you want to see your friend again," Robert yelled, "you better come back here!"

Then he saw the poacher swing his leg back and

kick Matt. Thud!

"Don't hurt me!" Matt yelped.

Clancy joined Robert. They stood over Matt, bears in a threatening posture, their necks arched downward.

Seth clenched his fists. What could he do?

If Quest was still alive, Seth thought, and not too far away, then he might have a plan. Maybe it could work. Yanking off his gloves and dropping them to the ground, he put two fingers to his mouth and whistled. He whistled again, more shrilly.

Seth squeezed his eyes tightly together. He whistled once more. This time, he heard Quest's familiar whinny and snorting response. Branches snapped as Quest galloped toward him, tossing his flaxen mane, his flaring nostrils a tender rose color. He skidded his muscular legs to a stop, nearly knocking Seth over.

"Remember barrel racing, boy?" Seth said as he jumped into the saddle. His hands were sweaty. His throat was dusty as dry leaves. He took a deep breath, leaned forward, and raced Quest back down the ravine and up the hill—straight toward the poachers. If he could get the men to move toward the mound that he'd nearly fallen through earlier . . .

Robert swung and sent Matt flying to the ground. He glanced up at Seth approaching. "I can't believe this!" he hollered, and reached for a large stick.

But before Robert was able to grab it, Seth charged straight at him, then leaned back in his saddle as he pulled up on the reins. Quest reared up, his hooves flailing the air above the poacher's head.

"Clancy!" Robert shouted, stumbling backward away from the horse. "Shoot it!"

"I left it . . . ," Clancy said, and started to run toward the slope in the direction of their four-wheeler, but Seth swerved his horse across the old man's path.

"Stupid kid!" Clancy shouted, and started into a coughing fit. "Gonna get . . . yourself killed!" he wheezed as Seth herded the old man straight toward Robert and the mound of debris.

Neck-reining to the left and right, Seth made tight turns around the men. Quest's pounding hooves churned the white snow to brown splotches. The men swore as they scrambled away from Quest's quick-moving hooves.

Seth hoped his plan would work. Robert tried to

grab at Seth's left boot, but Seth quickly spun Quest to the left, knocking Robert to the ground.

"You're gonna pay!" Robert shouted, scrambling toward Clancy.

Finally, making a tight circle around the edge of the decaying garbage mound, Seth forced the poachers to its center. With a sudden groan, the old timbers gave way, and the men disappeared into the shaft below.

Seth stared. He couldn't believe it! They were gone. His plan had actually worked.

Moaning floated up from the shaft.

At least he hadn't killed them.

"Hey!" Robert yelled, his voice less threatening. "C'mom, get us out of here! We won't bother you."

Seth's legs trembled as he slid off Quest to the ground. He draped his rubbery arms around Quest's neck. "Good boy," he said over and over. "Good boy, Quest."

Matt limped to Seth's side, his face ashen.

For a moment, they just stared at each other.

"I didn't expect you'd bring help so fast," Matt said.

A chopping sound fumbled in the distance, then quickly filled the air. The boys looked up.

A helicopter sailed over the treetops, blowing the nearby branches with its whir of propellers.

"Let's get out of here!" Seth yelled to Matt about the roar. "Quick, hop up. It's probably some of their friends coming in for a shipment."

Like an enormous wasp, the helicopter descended to the clearing below the hill. Speeding toward the copter on four-wheelers, two big men approached on the trail.

Just as Seth placed his foot in the stirrup, he heard a familiar voice.

"Seth!" his father shouted.

Seth yanked out his foot and turned. He dropped Quest's reins and ran to meet his dad coming up over the crest of the hill. "Dad!"

"Your mom radioed," he called. "She was worried about you. Now I find you here! You could get killed. Get home! Fast!"

"Wait," Seth said, pointing to the black hole of the vertical shaft. "I'll explain everything. There's a couple of guys—"

"This isn't the time for jokes," Dad warned. "Now get home!"

"But Dad! Clancy and Robert are down there!"

His dad looked toward the hole, then back at the

whirring helicopter.

"Dad, you've gotta believe me. Take a look!" Seth said, running back to the shaft. "They're unarmed," Seth said.

Dad's mouth was drawn in a firm line. He walked toward the dark cavity and looked down.

Seth called down. "Gentlemen, meet my dad, the game warden!"

Cursing boiled up from the pit below.

"Huh," Dad said, shaking his head. "I can't quite believe it. Clancy, even the Feds flew in to see you this time. Breaking the Lacey Act and going international caught their attention. Fellas, you're under arrest."

Then Dad stepped back from the hole. He yanked off his fake beard and moustache, put his hands on Seth's shoulders, and looked hard at Seth. "I don't know all you've been up to—I'm sure there's some foolishness in it—but what's important now is that you're all right. I don't know what I'd do if something had happened to you."

Seth threw his arms around Dad's chest, closed his eyes, and hugged him fiercely. "Dad, I'm—"

Suddenly he pulled away. "Oh! I almost forgot," he blurted. "The moose calf!"

CHAPTER SEVENTEEN

With his dad following, Seth ran through the birch trees, past the pile of bear carcasses, and on toward the creek bed, brambles cutting his numb hands and face. He stopped and listened for any sound of splashing or struggling. He heard only his own hard breathing.

At the edge of the water, he found the moose calf, motionless. Its arched brown muzzle rested on the ridge of ice; its close-set eyes were closed.

"No!" Seth said, shaking his head. "No! I'm too late!" He suddenly felt tired and heavy. He dropped to the edge of the creek bed and stared at the calf. "I was going to help you," he whispered.

Seth's dad came up from behind. "Poor animal," he said. "What a shame."

But as Seth looked more closely, the calf's soft nostrils flared, almost imperceptibly. Seth felt an ember of hope burst into a brilliant flare. "Dad, look!" he shouted. "It's still alive!"

With one end of the rope around his waist, Seth stretched across the plywood toward the moose calf and tied the other end around its neck. Together, he and his dad pulled the calf closer to shore, far enough out of the water so Seth could slip another rope under the calf's front legs.

Thundering overhead, the helicopter whipped the few remaining autumn leaves off branches, dropping them onto the frozen creek bed below. A white rope dropped from the passenger side of the copter into the nearby brush.

Seth grabbed the rope and knotted it around the calf's girth, just behind its front legs. He pulled on the ropes to make sure they'd hold, then stepped back and signaled with a wave to the helicopter.

Effortlessly, like a father scooping a child in his arms, the helicopter lifted the calf slowly upward, hovered for a second above the creek, then moved over the treetops toward the trail.

"Good work," Dad said, standing behind Seth.

Seth turned. "Thanks, but I'm not ready to take over your job, not yet anyway." For a second he beamed, and then he grew serious.

"Dad," he said, shuffling his feet uncomfortably, "we need to talk." He didn't want to shatter his dad's new respect for him, but he had to start being honest.

"Here?" Dad said with a mixture of laughter and irritation. "I'm sure it can wait till we get home. Ray's waiting." He pushed through the brush and began to walk away.

"Dad, I broke the law," Seth said loudly, his feet planted, "just like those poachers!"

Dad turned around and walked up to Seth. He raised his eyebrows. "You what?"

"I took out my shotgun without you," Seth said, eyes lowered. How could he look his dad in the eyes now? "That's when I came across the moose tracks for the first time—and I shot a rabbit."

Seth glanced up, waiting for Dad's blue eyes to cloud over, waiting for him to get angry, waiting for him to say something. Anything.

The helicopter droned in the distance.

"Well?" Seth said. "Don't you have to arrest me or something?"

The muscles around Dad's jaw tightened, then relaxed. Finally, he shook his head. "No," he said. "Doing what's right, like you just did, takes a whole lot more strength than it does to do what's wrong. If you want to know the truth, I'm proud of you. You've grown up a lot without my realizing it." He paused and rubbed his gloved hand across his unshaven face. "I think, Seth, that with all you've been through, you've already paid a pretty hefty penalty. What do you say?"

Seth didn't know what to say. He felt a sense of wholeness, of being complete, as though he'd passed a different kind of test than he'd expected. With his throat feeling constricted, he didn't try to answer. He just nodded to his Dad and smiled.

When they got back to the four-wheelers, Matt and Ray had already secured the calf from the helicopter into the poachers' trailer. Its legs were folded beneath it, its head drooped across the front edge, eyes closed. Seth walked over to it and cautiously touched its coarse wet hair.

He glanced at Dad, who was standing next to

Ray, arms crossed over his chest. He gave Seth a thumbs-up.

Ray scratched his chin. "Hard to believe," he said, "that those guys could make thousands of dollars selling gallbladders for cure-alls and love potions."

"Remember that alert a few years back," Dad said, "about a possible shipping connection from here to New York, then on to Korea?"

Ray nodded.

"At first," Dad said, "we didn't take it seriously. It sounded too far-fetched to be true. Gradually, however, the pieces started coming together. We just couldn't crack their operation," he said with a smile, "that is, until now."

Matt winked at Seth, then hobbled to the four-wheeler, trying to ease his leg over the seat.

Seth rushed over. "Here, let me help," he said, reaching for Matt's boot and gently lifting it over the seat.

Matt grimaced from the pain.

"Are you up to driving this back?" Seth asked quickly. "Do you think you can make it?"

Matt leveled a glare at Seth. "Quit being a mother hen, Seth. After all we've been through, you're asking . . ."

Seth put both hands up, surrendering. "Hey, you can make it, I don't have any doubt."

"Just follow close, okay?" Matt said, and started the motor.

Seth grabbed Quest's reins, slid his boot into the stirrup, and climbed into the saddle.

"Matt," Dad called over the engine's rumble, "better get your leg x-rayed, just in case it's fractured. And you guys," he added, "back the trailer up to the stall, but be careful. Remember, you're still dealing with a wild animal. Go ahead, Seth, and call the vet."

"Sure," Seth answered.

"I'll be home after we get these guys to jail," Dad said, glancing up to hill. "My guess is they're not in any hurry to start serving their time, probably up to twenty years each."

Seth waved, then headed Quest down the trail behind the four-wheeler.

Quest's steady pace and rocking motion helped quiet Seth down inside. He kept his eyes on the chocolaty brown calf only a few feet ahead. He'd actually done it: he'd helped the calf. Though it hardly moved, Seth prayed that a warm barn, some water and grain, would revive it. He'd do everything he could to help it regain its strength.

As they neared the ancient, towering Hercules, Seth stopped his horse and let Matt motor ahead.

CHAPTER EIGHTEEN

Seth reached into his jacket pocket and pulled out the silky rabbit's foot. He stared at the paw in his open hand, then clasped it again and dropped off his horse to the ground.

The snow crunched as he stepped over the far-reaching roots of the enormous pine. Squatting down, he scooped out a small bowl of snow and gently placed the rabbit's foot in the hollow.

"Rabbit," he said aloud, "maybe you can't hear me, but I'm sorry I wasted your life. At least I learned a lesson." For a few moments, he was still. Then silently, he covered the paw with snow.

Seth looked up through the branches of the pine tree, breathed in the fresh forest air, and listened to the chatter of two red squirrels as they chased each other around and around the trunk of the towering pine, climbing ever higher toward the cluster of brown cones adorning the top.

Windows of blue opened up between the clouds. A flock of goldeneye ducks flew overhead in V formation, heading south before winter completely sheeted the lakes with ice and once again tossed her white quilt over the land.

As the flock disappeared on the horizon, Seth walked back to the trail.

He ran his fingers through Quest's warm winter coat. Then he swung his leg up into the saddle, clicked his tongue, and cantered toward home.